This
PJ BOOK
belongs to

PJ Library®

JEWISH BEDTIME STORIES and SONGS

For Ruby Dew, our little rainbow

Text copyright © Jim Coplestone 2004
Illustrations copyright © Lis Coplestone 2004

The rights of Jim Coplestone to be identified as the author and of Lis Coplestone
to be identified as the illustrator of this Work have been asserted by them in accordance
with the Copyright, Designs and Patents Act, 1988.

First published in Great Britain in 2004 by
Frances Lincoln Children's Books, 74-77 White Lion Street
London, N1 9PF

www.franceslincoln.com

First paperback edition published in 2005

British Library Cataloguing in Publication Data available on request

071824.7K3/B528/A3

ISBN 978-1-84780-581-2

Printed in China

3 5 7 9 8 6 4 2

Noah's Bed

Lis and Jim Coplestone

F

FRANCES LINCOLN
CHILDREN'S BOOKS

Eber helped Grandpa Noah
and Grandma Nora to build a huge Ark,
to keep their family and a pair
of every kind of animal safe
when the big flood came.

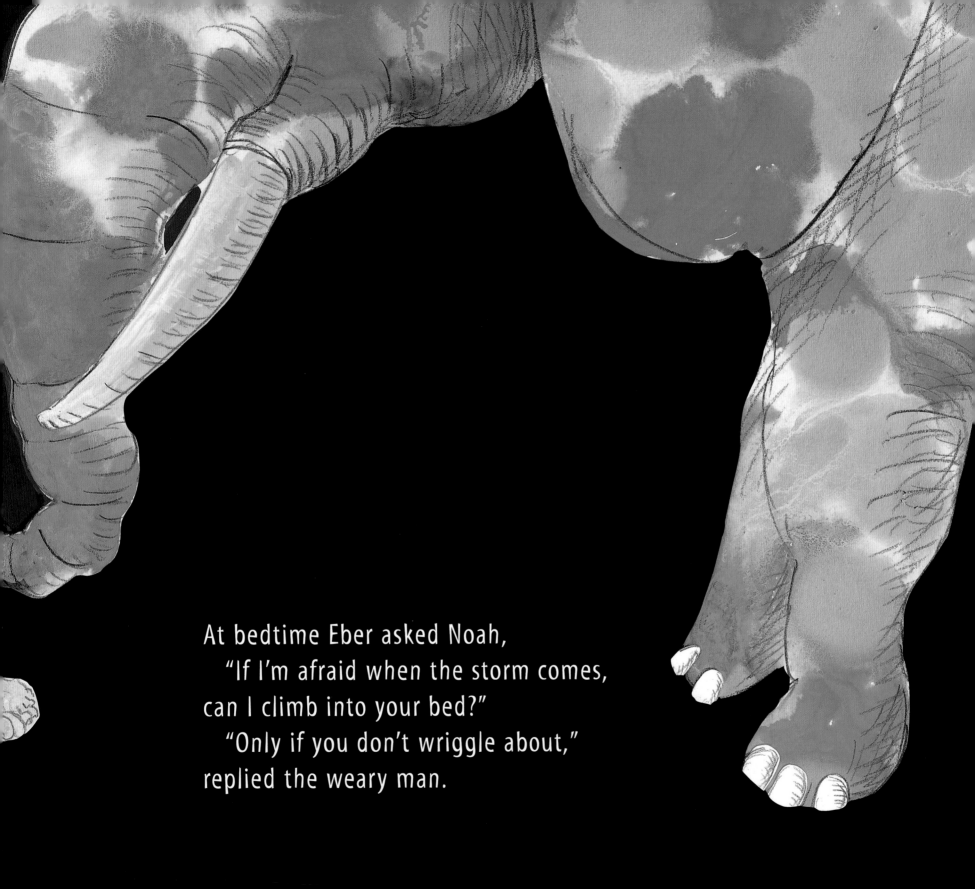

At bedtime Eber asked Noah,
 "If I'm afraid when the storm comes,
can I climb into your bed?"
 "Only if you don't wriggle about,"
replied the weary man.

The rain fell.
The water rose.
The Ark rocked like a giant cradle
and lulled Eber and all the animals to sleep.

"Good night, every two," Noah whispered.

All was calm inside the Ark,
but outside the storm was gathering.
Wild winds stirred among the clouds.
The birds of paradise woke up in a terrible flap.

A bright forked tongue of lightning flickered.
The scaly green iguanas woke up and shivered with fear.

The wind howled around the Ark
and woke the lions.
They twitched in alarm
from their neat whiskers
to their straggly tail-tips.

Thunder stampeded across the sky.
Even the hefty elephants were frightened
by that fearful earful.

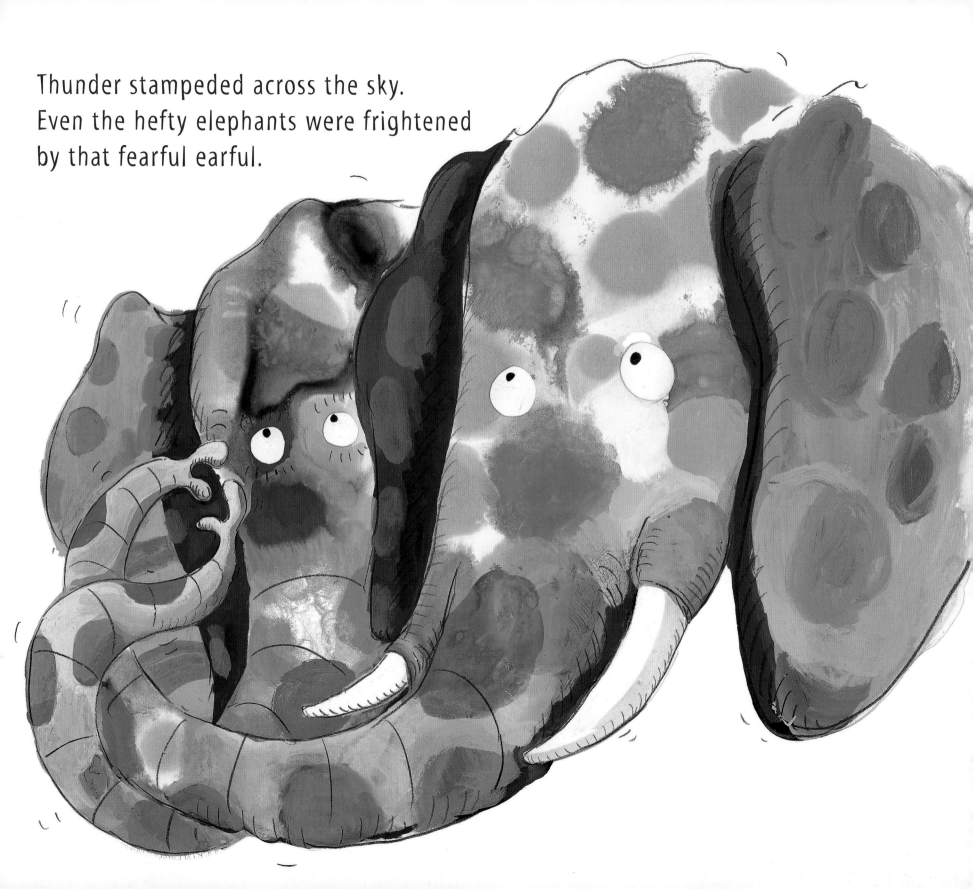

A gigantic CRACK of thunder
made Eber sit up.
In a flash, he was creeping through
the dark Ark, to his grandparents' bed.

"Cuddle me up, Grandpa, I'm scared!"
the little boy mumbled into Noah's huge beard.
"All right, but remember, no wriggling!" whispered Noah.
Eber and his grandparents snuggled down
to sleep again and all was peaceful aboard the Ark.

But then...

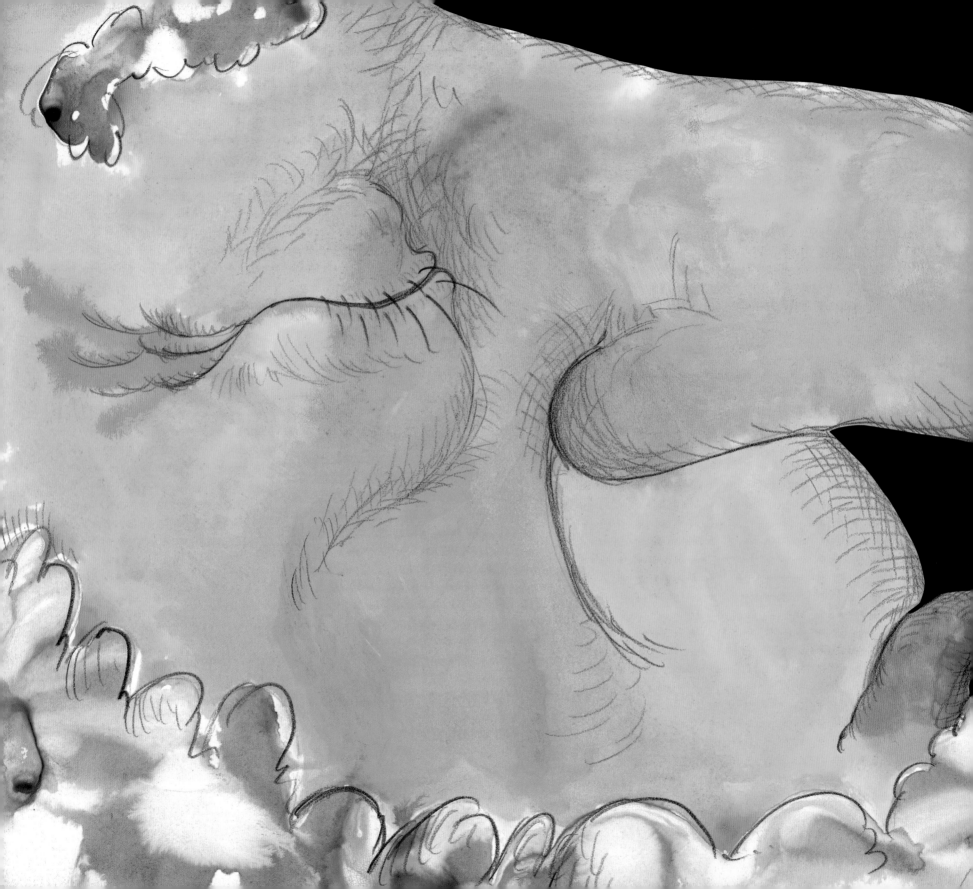

something tickled Noah's nose.
  "Aawfff," he grumbled.
"Your hair is tickly, Eber.
Please stop fidgeting and go to sleep."
  But then...

something scratched Nora's leg.
"Aaaagh!" she squawked.
"I must cut your toenails, Eber.
Do try to keep still, dear."
But then...

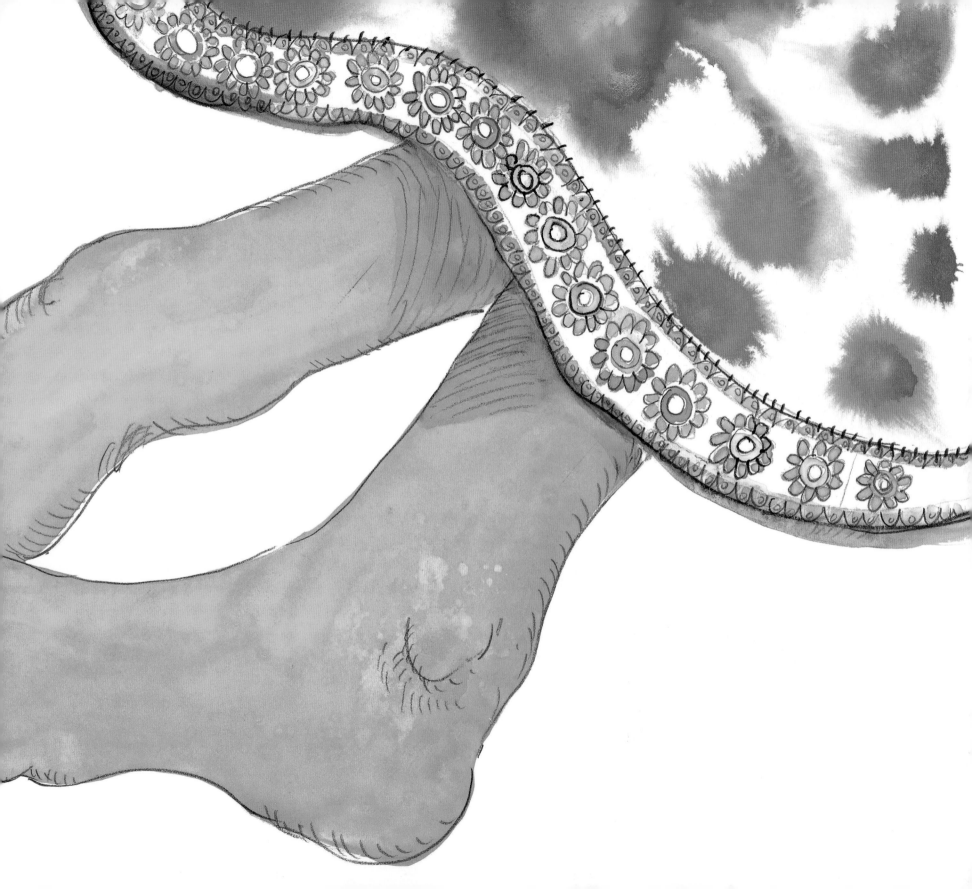

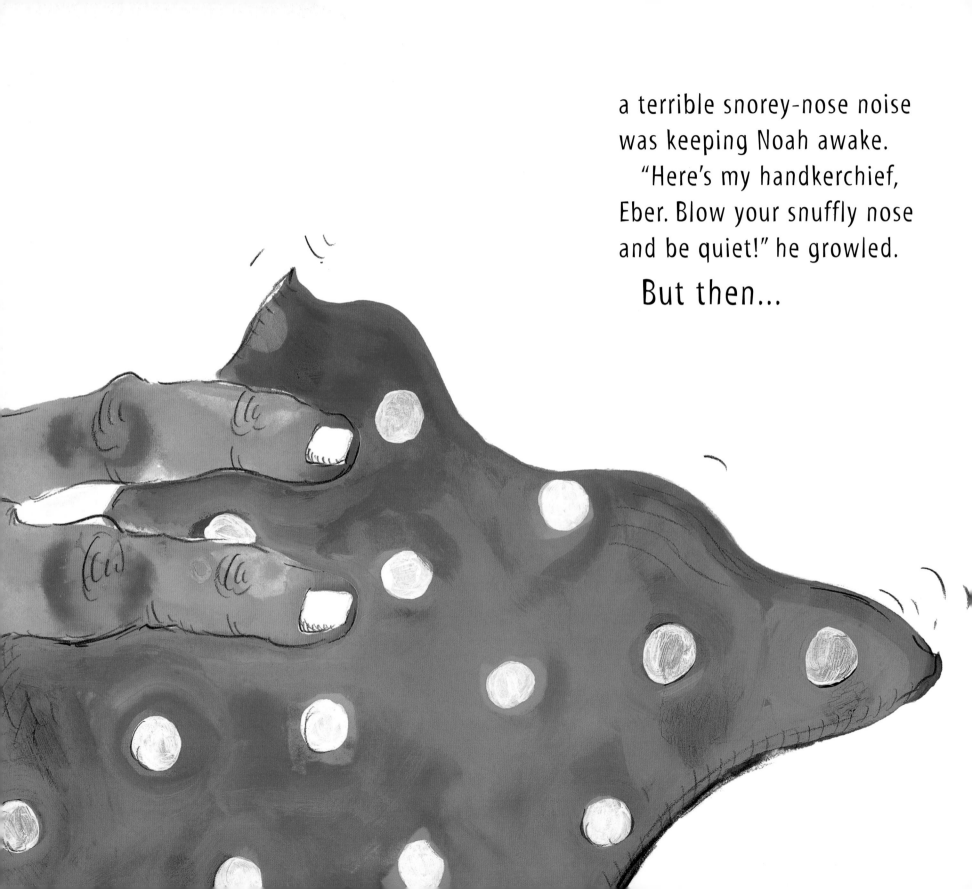

a terrible snorey-nose noise
was keeping Noah awake.
"Here's my handkerchief,
Eber. Blow your snuffly nose
and be quiet!" he growled.

But then...

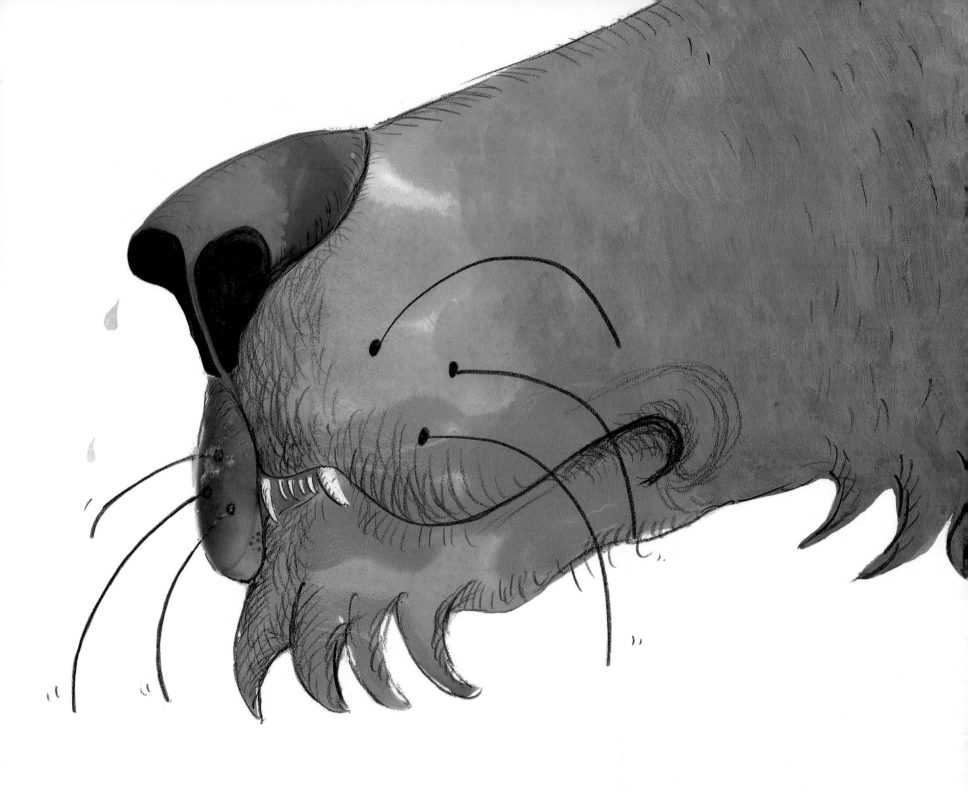

Noah and Nora were suddenly
very chilly.
    "Brrrrrrr!" shivered Nora.
"Do you have to take up
so much of the quilt, Eber?"

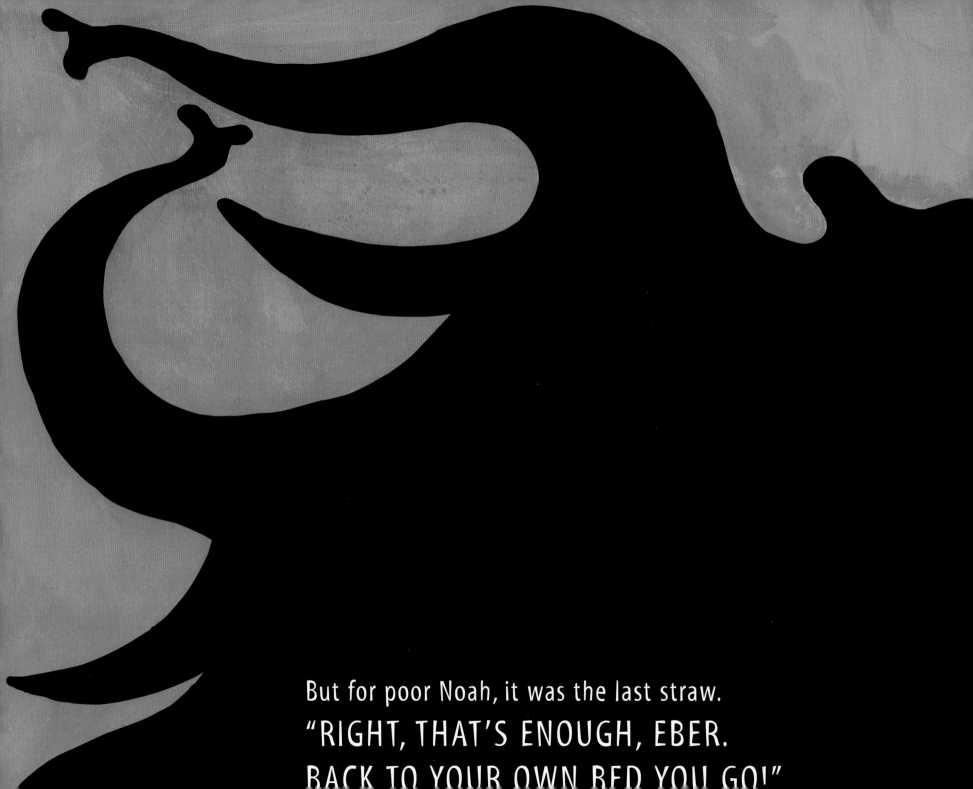

But for poor Noah, it was the last straw.
"RIGHT, THAT'S ENOUGH, EBER.
BACK TO YOUR OWN BED YOU GO!"

He struck a match and lit the lamp...

and there in the bed were...

two tickly birds of paradise,
two scratchy green iguanas,
two snorey-nose lions,
two hefty elephants...

and Eber who was fast asleep.